DARK HUNTER

THE FACE IN THE FOREST

WITHDRAWN

First published 2015 by
A & C Black, an imprint of Bloomsbury Publishing Plc
50 Bedford Square, London, WC1B 3DP

www.bloomsbury.com

A CIP catalogue for this book is available from the British Library

ISBN: 978–1–4729–0825–4

Typeset by Newgen Knowledge Works (P) Ltd., Chennai, India
Printed and bound in Great Britain by CPI Group (UK) Ltd,
Croydon CR0 4YY

1 3 5 7 9 10 8 6 4 2

recommended by

www.catchup.org

Catch Up is a not-for-profit charity
which aims to address the problem of
underachievement that has its roots in
literacy and numeracy difficulties.

DARK HUNTER

THE FACE IN THE FOREST

BENJAMIN HULME-CROSS

ILLUSTRATED BY NELSON EVERGREEN

A & C BLACK
AN IMPRINT OF BLOOMSBURY
LONDON   NEW DELHI   NEW YORK   SYDNEY

The Dark Hunter

Mr Daniel Blood is the Dark Hunter.
People call him to fight evil demons,
vampires and ghosts.

Edgar and Mary help Mr Blood
with his work.

The three hunters need to be strong and
clever to survive…

Contents

Chapter 1

Lord Gray

Mr Blood rang the doorbell at a large manor house. Edgar and Mary heard heavy footsteps. Slowly, the door was opened by an old servant.

I am the Dark Hunter," said Mr Blood. "We are here to see Lord Gray."

"Follow me," the man replied.

Lord Gray had written to Mr Blood and asked him to take his daughter on a journey.

The old man led them into a huge room. At the far end of the room stood a tall, thin man. He was staring up at a huge painting on the wall. Mary giggled. The man was staring at a painting of himself.

"This is Mr Blood," said the old man, and left the room.

Lord Gray asked his three guests to sit. "Thank you for coming," he said. "I have a very important task for you. My step-daughter, Anna, is to be married to Lord Burkett."

Lord Gray pointed to the corner of the room. Edgar saw a girl not much older than himself. She stood by the window, looking out.

"It has taken me years to find her a husband," said Lord Gray. "We are lucky that we found anyone willing to marry her!"

"Willing to pay for me, you mean," said the girl.

"Be quiet!" Lord Gray snapped. "Young women should be seen and not heard. I am glad to be rid of her at last."

Mary gave Lord Gray a nasty look.
Mr Blood said nothing but Edgar could tell
that he was angry.

"Lord Burkett's castle is on the other side of the forest," said Lord Gray. "The only way to get there is to follow the path through the trees and it is a three-day ride. I would take her myself but I do not like long trips. Also, I hear that you are able to guard against… things of the night."

Mary and Edgar looked at each other. Now they knew why Lord Gray had written to Mr Blood.

"People say that spirits live in the forest," said Lord Gray. "That's all nonsense, of course. But Anna must reach Lord Burkett safely."

"He won't pay you until I get there," said Anna.

"Be quiet, girl!" shouted Lord Gray.

Mr Blood stared at Lord Gray. He didn't like the way Lord Gray treated Anna. "Will you take the job?" asked Lord Gray.

Mr Blood nodded his head.

"Good!" said Lord Gray. "You will leave in the morning. A new life for you, Anna!"

Anna turned and stared out of the window again.

Chapter 2

Into the Forest

They set off at dawn. They rode along a narrow road for many hours. Late in the afternoon the road became a track and they entered the green gloom of a huge forest.

Mr Blood rode at the front, followed by Edgar. Mary and Anna were at the back.

Edgar didn't like the gloom of the forest but Anna looked much happier once they were riding through the trees.

"You must be glad to get away from Lord Gray," said Mary.

Anna nodded. "All he thinks about is how to get his hands on more money."

Edgar heard a rustle off to one side of the track.

"What was that?" he asked, nervously.

"Probably just a rabbit," laughed Anna.

"Lord Gray would never let me come riding in the forest." Anna told Mary. "But I love it here. Sometimes I would sneak off on my own."

Anna smiled. "When I was little I used to pretend there was a giant in the forest and that he was my friend. I felt safe in the forest because I knew my friend would protect me," she said.

The rustling began again.

"Listen!" said Edgar. "There's something out there."

"It's probably just the wind in the trees," said Anna.

Edgar didn't reply. He was wanted to say that there was no wind but he didn't want the girls to think he was frightened.

Suddenly, Mr Blood stopped. They all looked ahead. In front of them was a dead tree with a large hole in it. In the hole was what looked like a huge human face, carved out of wood. Edgar looked round at the girls. Anna had turned very pale.

Edgar turned back to look at the carved head.

It blinked.

Suddenly, all four horses reared up, wild with terror. As their hooves came crashing back down, they bolted.

Everyone clung on desperately. The horses galloped deeper and deeper into the forest. By the time the horses slowed down, Mr Blood and the children were completely lost.

Chapter 3

Tor

The horses had stopped beside a pool.
Edgar and Mary were pale and shaking
and Mr Blood looked grim but Anna
looked excited.

"There's nothing to be happy about," snapped Edgar. "We're lost!"

"But this place is just so… exciting!" said Anna.

Mary giggled. She thought Anna was good fun.

The last light of the day was disappearing. They had no idea where they were or how to find the track again. Edgar couldn't see why the two girls were so cheerful.

"I suppose we'll have to spend the night here," said Edgar. Mr Blood agreed. Edgar tied up the horses and Mr Blood began making a shelter for the night.

"Let's make a fire," said Mary. She and Anna went to get dry wood.

Edgar walked to the edge of the pool.
He stared into it and thought about the
giant face they had seen back on the path.
The face had been real and it had moved.
The horses had seen it too.

But Anna's face had turned white *before* the face in the tree had blinked. That was strange. Edgar looked over at Anna. She was sitting by the fire laughing and talking to Mary. She didn't seem afraid.

"Food," Mr Blood called out. Edgar walked over to the fire and sat down beside Mary. For a while they ate the bread and cheese in silence.

"We all saw it," said Edgar at last. "What was it?"

"A forest giant," said Mr Blood. "I've heard of them but I've never seen one before."

"I have," said Anna, suddenly. "I've seen this one before. He's called Tor."

Edgar and Mary looked surprised.

"Tell us more," said Mr Blood, looking at Anna.

"When I was little, " said Anna, " I used to creep out of the house and come into the forest. Tor talked to me. As I got older, I stopped going to the forest and I forgot about Tor. Or I forgot about him being real. I thought he was part of a pretend game in my head. But when I saw that face… I knew it was him."

"Should we be afraid?" Mary asked.

"You don't need to be afraid of Tor." Anna replied. " He used to say he would always protect me from harm."

"But what if he thinks *we* mean you harm…" said Edgar.

"You're right," Mr Blood said to Edgar. "We could be in danger. Forest giants don't come looking for trouble. They stay hidden. But they are still giants . . ."

Beyond the firelight the forest was now in total darkness. The screeches and growls of the night animals filled the air. The horses snorted as they chewed the grass.

A moment later, Edgar frowned. "Listen," he hissed.

"I can't hear anything," said Mary.

"Yes," Edgar said. "That's the problem."

The forest had fallen silent.

Chapter 4

The Trees

For a few moments they waited. Then the horses panicked. They tore at the ropes and broke loose, and charged away into the blackness of the forest.

"What's going on?" Edgar wailed.

Suddenly, Mary screamed, "Get it off me!"

Something was slowly pulling Mary by the ankle away from the fire. Mr Blood grabbed his axe and leapt after her. He swung the axe and cut through something on the ground near Mary's foot.

"It's the trees," he hissed, pulling Mary back to the others. "They're trying to kill us. Get in between the fire and the pool."

Mr Blood was right. A tree root had twisted itself around Mary's ankle. Mr Blood lit a few torches and planted them in the ground.

Now, they were protected by the water
on one side and the torches on the other.

"Will that keep them back?" asked
Edgar.

"Trees don't like fire," said Mr Blood.
But the trees were all moving now.

Roots slid across the ground towards
them. They hissed when they got close to
the fire.

The roots made darting jabs forward but then pulled back. More roots began to pile up forming a wall around the ring of torches.

"We're safe for now," said Mr Blood. "They won't come past the fire."

Edgar felt something wet on his feet, and looked down. He shouted in alarm. "Water! The water! It's rising!"

Anna screamed. The pool was getting bigger, creeping out to meet the trees. It rose around their ankles. The fire went out with a loud hiss as the water reached it. The tree roots jabbed towards them as the water rose.

"What do we do?" cried Mary. But Mr Blood had no answer. The first of the torches hissed and died, and Anna screamed again.

Suddenly, a huge roar filled the forest. The tree roots shook.

And then the forest giant appeared. His great face was twisted with rage. His eyes were shiny and black. He wore a great cloak of mosses and vines that rustled when he moved. He roared again, and grabbed the nearest tree. He tore it out of the ground by the trunk and flung it over the tops of the trees next to it.

The water stopped rising. The tree roots stopped moving.

Then the roots began to slide backwards towards the trees. The water level began to fall.

"He's saving us!" cried Anna. "Thank you, Tor! You said you would protect me!"

When the roots had gone, the giant looked down at the group. "Anna," he boomed. "Why are you here with these strangers?"

"They are my friends," said Anna. "Lord Gray has asked them to take me to Lord Burkett's castle on the other side of the forest."

"Why?" asked the giant.

"To be married," said Anna.

"And is that what you want?" the giant asked.

"I don't know," Anna whispered.

"Then stay in the forest with me until you decide," said the giant.

"But what if Lord Gray comes looking for her?" asked Mary.

Tor's huge face broke into a smile. "We will be ready for him," he laughed.

And Mary and Edgar heard all the tree roots rustle as if they were laughing too.